ELEPHANTS CAN'T JUMP

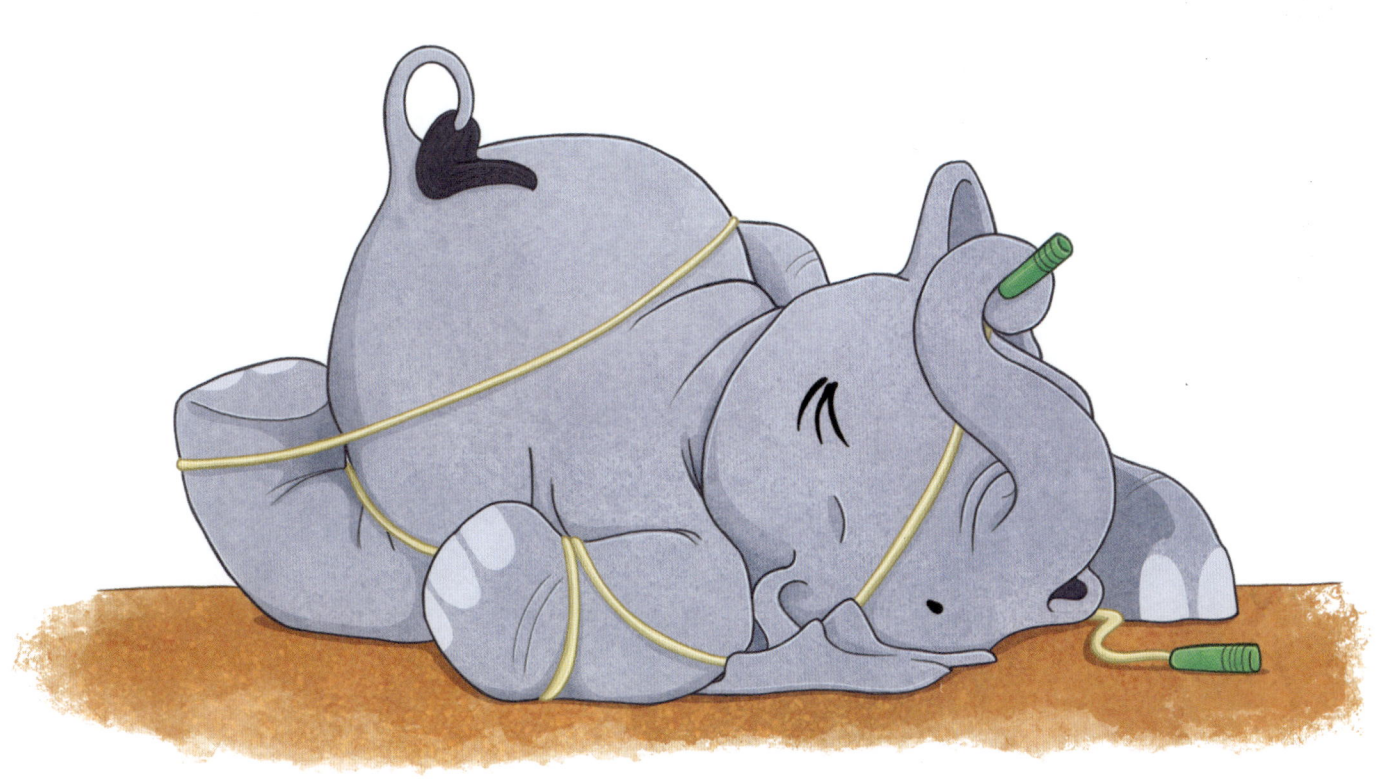

To the original Mini, for teaching me that a lost voice can always be found

– Venita

For Margaret-the-magnificent-Mother-in-Law, who always jumps in and lends a hand

– Natashia

Mini and Milo: Elephants Can't Jump
Walker Books Australia Pty Ltd
Locked Bag 22, Newtown
NSW 2042 Australia
www.walkerbooks.com.au

Walker Books Australia acknowledges the Traditional Owners of the country on which we work, the Gadigal and Wangal peoples of the Eora Nation, and recognizes their continuing connection to the land, waters and culture. We pay our respect to their Elders past and present.

The moral rights of the author and illustrator have been asserted.

Text © 2025 Venita Dimos
Illustrations © 2025 Natashia Curtin

All rights reserved. No part of this publication may be reproduced, stored in a retrieval system, or transmitted in any form or by any means – electronic, mechanical, photocopying, recording or otherwise – without the prior written permission of the publisher.

A catalogue record for this book is available from the National Library of Australia

ISBN: 978 1 7616 0075 3

The illustrations for this book were created digitally
Typeset in Ovo, with Blue Sheep, Bokka and Nippon Note
Printed and bound in China

10 9 8 7 6 5 4 3 2 1

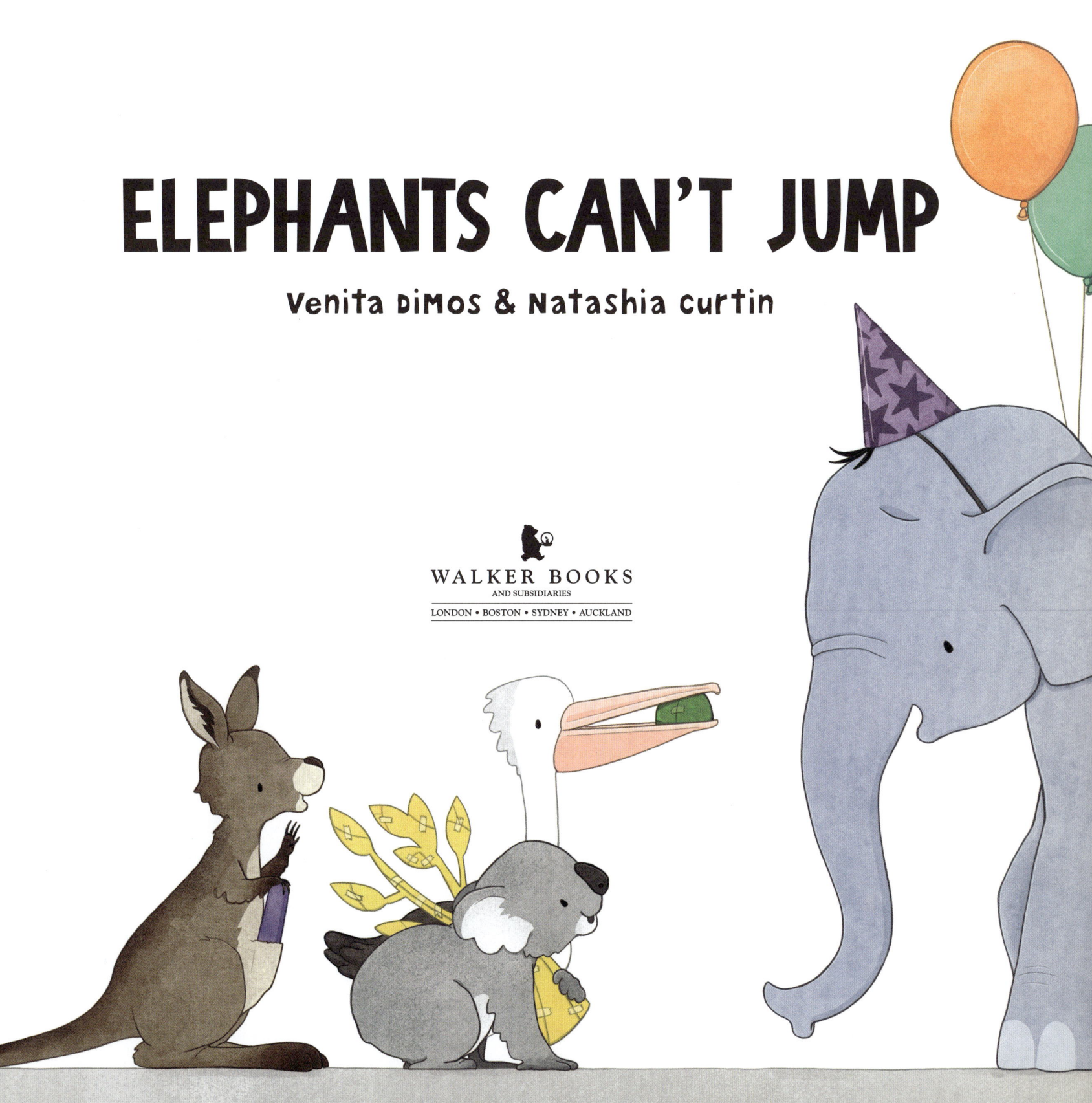

ELEPHANTS CAN'T JUMP

Venita Dimos & Natashia Curtin

WALKER BOOKS
AND SUBSIDIARIES
LONDON • BOSTON • SYDNEY • AUCKLAND

It had been the best birthday **ever**.
And Mini's **favorite** part had just begun . . .
Opening her presents!
Mini had saved the best present for last.

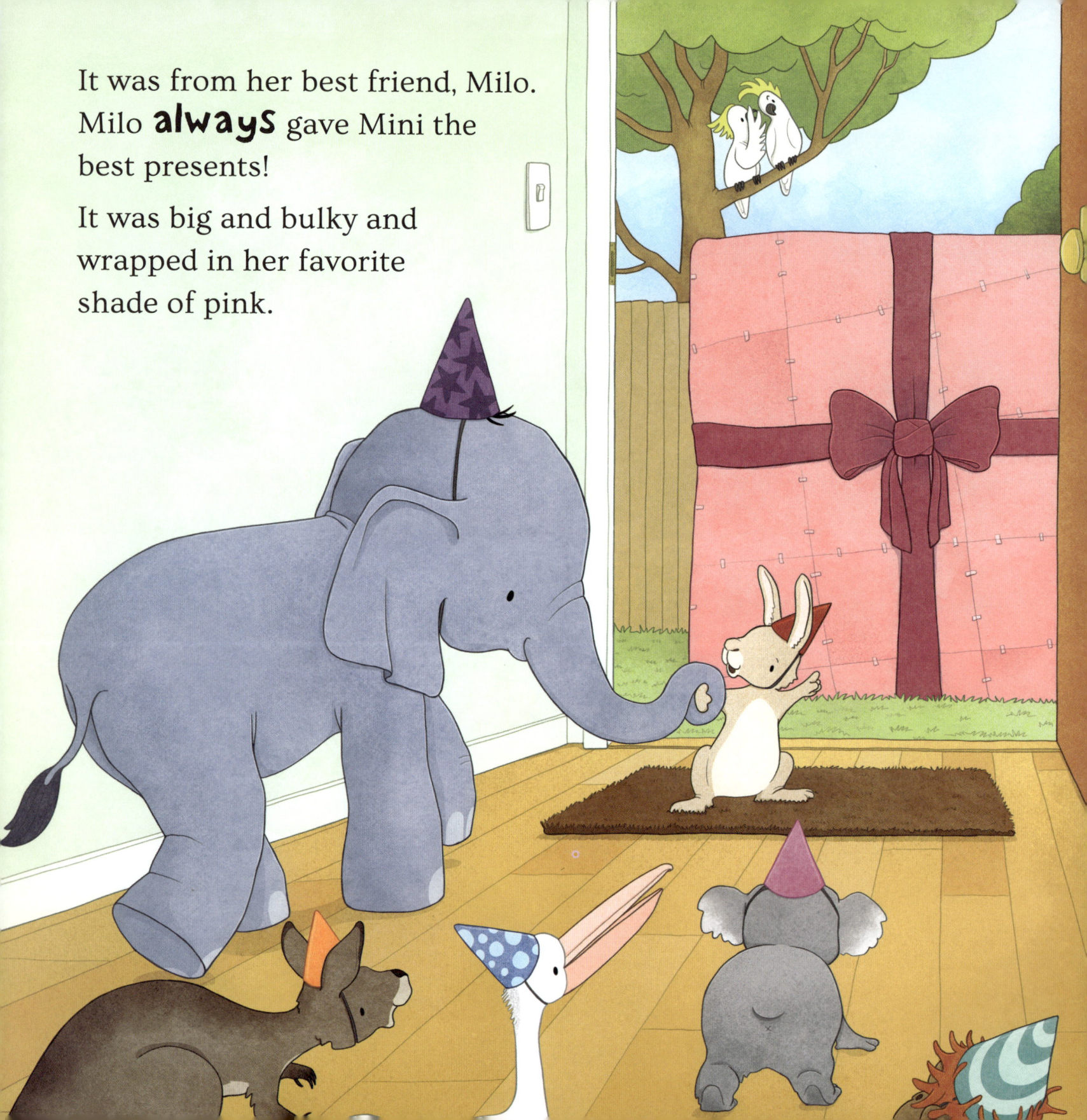

It was from her best friend, Milo. Milo **always** gave Mini the best presents!

It was big and bulky and wrapped in her favorite shade of pink.

Mini tore off the paper,
her trunk wild with wonder,
her heart thumping loudly.

And then she saw it.

It was **big** and **bright**, colorful and **bouncy**, **springy** and **hoppy**. It was a . . .

An angry fireball grew in Mini's head.
How could Milo do this to me? thought Mini.
It was the worst present ever! Milo should know . . .

Elephants can't jump!

"What's wrong, Mini?" asked Milo.

But Mini did not feel like talking. **"Nothing,"** grunted Mini.

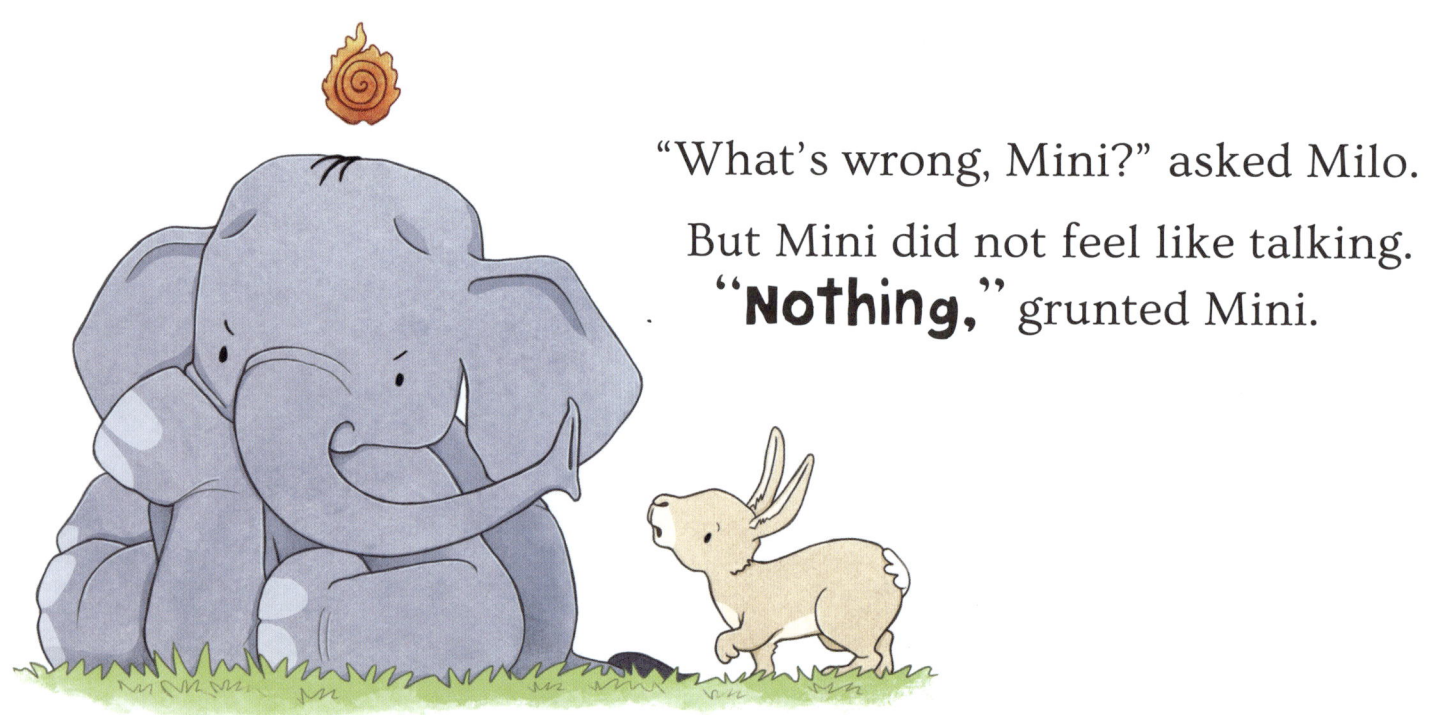

The next morning, the angry fireball was **still** there. "Come play with me, Mini!" said Milo.

But Milo was playing . . .

Hopscotch!!

How could Milo do this to me? thought Mini.

She couldn't play **hopscotch!**

Milo should know . . .
Elephants can't jump!

"Mini, what's wrong?" asked Milo.

"**Nothing,**" grunted Mini.

Mini's angry fireball was getting **bigger** and **bigger**.

But talking to Milo just felt too hard.

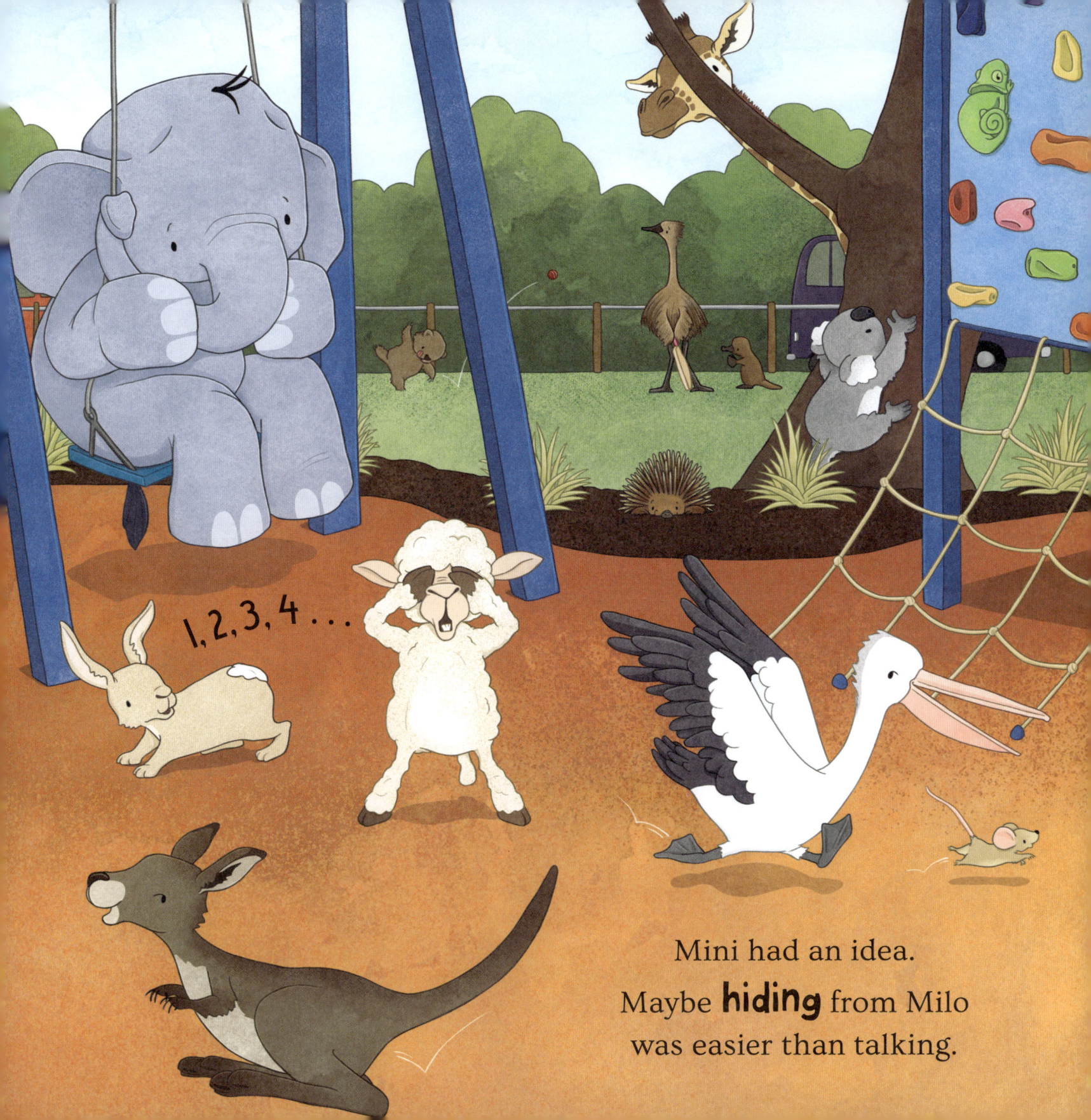

1, 2, 3, 4 ...

Mini had an idea.
Maybe **hiding** from Milo was easier than talking.

She hid behind the tallest tree.

And then underneath the biggest slide.

She even tried burying herself in the sand.

But hiding is **hard** when you're an elephant.

Maybe **running away** from Milo was easier.

On Monday, Mini **ran** home from school.

On Tuesday, she **sprinted** home after basketball practice.

On Wednesday she **bolted** home from the shops.

And on Thursday, Mini realized rabbits can run faster than elephants . . .

Because whenever she came home,
Milo would be waiting for her.

Running away hadn't solved anything,
it only made her feel **exhausted**.

Milo was feeling more and more puzzled by Mini's behavior, so on Friday, he asked Mini to come to his house and play.

Even though Mini was still mad at Milo, she decided to go. After all, Milo **always** had scrumptious food.

But when Mini arrived, she saw it. A **big** and **bright**, **colorful** and **bouncy**, **springy** and **hoppy** . . .

Jumping castle?

Mini had had **enough!**
But she was too tired to run.
She was too tired to hide.

She buried her head in her ears.

"What's wrong, Mini?" asked Milo, looking more puzzled than ever.

"You know!" said Mini.
"No I **don't!**" said Milo.

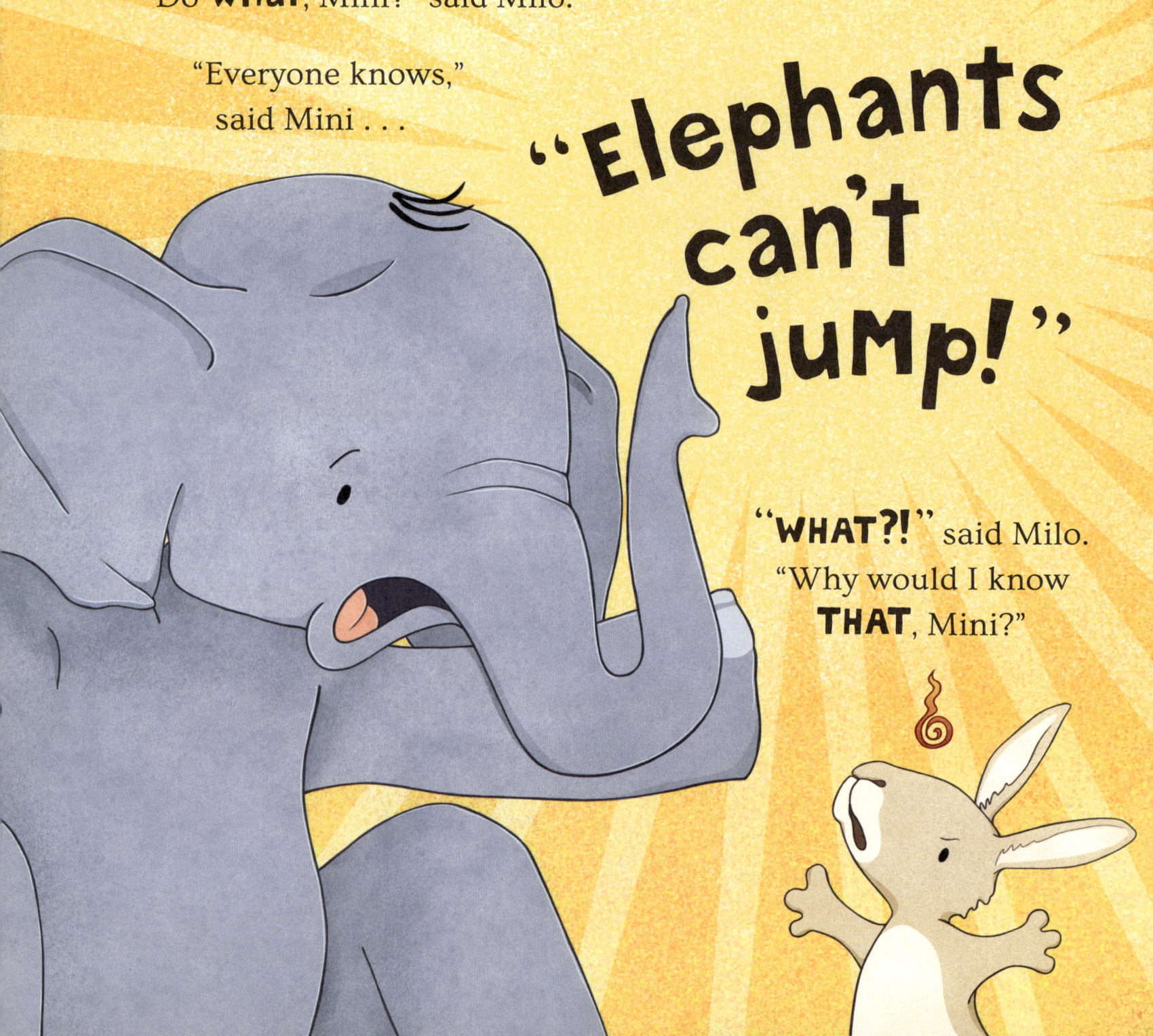

Just then, Mini realized that all this time...
she **thought** Milo knew why she was upset.
She **thought** Milo knew why she was angry.
But she had never **told** him.

It turns out that talking was **much** easier than running and hiding after all.

"Do you know what elephants **can** do with jumping castles Milo?" asked Mini.